My Dearest Dido
The Holodomor Story

Marion Mutala

Wood Dragon Books

My Dearest Dido – The Holodomor Story

Copyright 2019 Marion Mutala

Inside and cover art: Olha Tkachenko

Photo of Marion Mutala: Bruce Blom

ISBN:
Print (Paperback): 978-1-989078-09-9

Published by:
Wood Dragon Books
PO Box 429
Mossbank, Saskatchewan S0H 3G0
1-306-591-7993
www.WoodDragonBooks.com

Cataloguing and Publication Data available from Library and Archives Canada

Note: Three different fonts have been used to differentiate the three voices (letters from Hanusia to Dido, letters from Dido to his granddaughter, and entries to Dear Diary from Hanusia)

Praise for *My Dearest Dido*

"This book brings an important historical story to vivid life. It's heartbreaking, touching and necessary reading. A tale that artfully bridges the gap between the generations."

Arthur Slade, Author of **Crimson** *and* **Megiddo's Shadow**

"No Holodomor or genocide should ever happen; it is inhumanity to humanity by humanity. We cannot undo the Holodomor perpetrated against Ukrainians and other peoples of the former Soviet Union. However, we must not allow this terrible event to remain forgotten. Marion's book allows a younger generation of children to be informed about this horrific happening not just as a statistical or historical fact but an event that hurt people and destroyed families. This book explains the Holodomor in a language and context that children can relate to. May this book serve to educate and sensitize the next generation to strive for peace and dignity among all people."

Dr. Bill Gulka, Professor, University of Saskatchewan

Other books by Marion Mutala

Children's Books
Baba's Babushka: A Magical Ukrainian Christmas
Baba's Babushka: A Magical Ukrainian Easter
Baba's Babushka: A Magical Ukrainian Wedding
Kohkum's Babushka: A Magical Métis/Ukrainian Tale
Grateful
More Babas, Please!
My Buddy, Dido!

Poetry
Ukrainian Daughter's Dance

Fiction
The Time for Peace Is Now

DEDICATION

To the millions of voices from the Ukrainian genocide
and to the *Holodomor* survivors and their families.
Your story is told.
You are not forgotten!

Table of Contents

"Wake up Taras and look around you.
Not a cow or pig in sight,
nor a morsel to eat,
Only Stalin's portrait on the wall."

N. Mychajlowska, A *Holodomor* Survivor

From the Author

I was asked by Dr. Bill Gulka to consider writing a book about the *Holodomor*, the Ukrainian genocide. Initially, I did not think I could do this as the *Holodomor* is such a difficult subject to research, let alone write. Then an idea came to me, perhaps by the Holy Spirit, of how to proceed with this horrific part of Ukrainian history. Through letters between Dido Bohdan and his granddaughter Hanka (or Hanusia as her grandfather liked to call her) and by Hanka's own diary entries - the story unfolds.

I present to you, *My Dearest Dido - The Holodomor Story*. My heart and soul were poured into writing this book as I tried to share this part of history accurately. If there are any flaws, they are unintentional.

From my *Holodomor* research, I decided to create two people to illustrate what happened during the *Holodomor*. The main fictional characters in this story, Bohdan and Hanka, are based on documented accounts of survivors' stories.

How did I come up with their names? Jennie Franko is my second cousin and her aunt Hanka lived through the *Holodomor* period. Hanka Klimochka (née-Hrabowa), Jennie Franko's mother's sister, was born in 1910 in the village of Perespa, Sokal - now Ukraine. I have used Jennie's aunt's name, Hanka Klimochka, and her aunt Hanka's family members' names not only to remember and honour her family but also as a representation of actual lives lost or affected by the *Holodomor*.

In the Ukrainian language, the name Bohdan means "gift from God." I feel it is an appropriate name for a survivor. His character is not named after one survivor but based on stories from many survivors. In this story, Bohdan uses many Ukrainian terms of endearment for his granddaughter such as *holubka, kalyna, soloveyko, sertse*. In Ukrainian, *Baba* is the name for grandmother and *Dido* is the name for grandfather.

My fictional Dido lives in Hafford, Saskatchewan, which was the hometown of my grandparents. My fictional Hanusia lives in Saskatoon, Saskatchewan, which is my hometown.

Marion Mutala

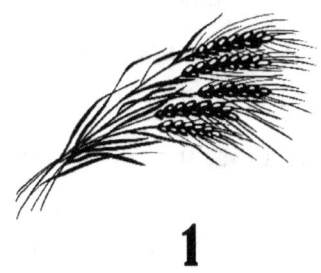

1

September 5

My Dearest Dido,

Grandpa, today I was told about the *Holodomor*. My teacher, Mrs. Dara, showed our class a picture of starving people. It was gross and disturbing. Mrs. Dara says *"holod"* in Ukrainian means hunger or famine and *"moryty"* means death or to torment. We practiced how to say it.

I chose to make the *Holodomor* the topic for my history essay. In my research, I was shocked to hear about the deliberate starvation of so many Ukrainians by Stalin during the years of this Ukrainian genocide. I found out that at the peak of the *Holodomor*, it's estimated 28,000 Ukrainian villagers died per day – 1,000 people per hour or seventeen per minute. One third of the deaths were children. Many more children were left orphaned or homeless. Children died first, then the men, and then the women. That's crazy!

When I came home from school, I asked my mother if this was true. Mom said you're a survivor of the *Holodomor*. She told me to ask you about it and suggested I write to you as it's such a difficult subject to talk about over the phone.

Is what my teacher told me true, Dido? Please tell me about the *Holodomor*. Did you really live through what they call the Ukrainian genocide? Were you one of the orphans left homeless?

Your loving granddaughter,
Hanka

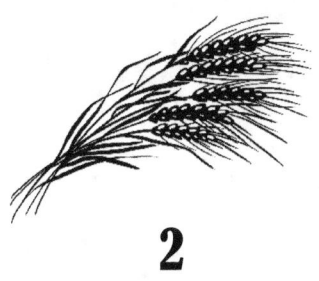

2

September 10

Dear Hanusia, my holubka,

Tak, that is right. Your teacher is correct. I was only eight years old at the time of the *Holodomor*. It is believed more people died in this Ukrainian genocide than any other genocide in world history. No exact figure is known but it is believed about **10,000,000** people died, of which **3,000,000** were children.

However, my little holubka, I do not wish to talk about this tragedy. It was a very painful part of my life. My heart is full of grave sorrow.

Love,
Dido

3

September 15

My Dearest Dido,

I love you so much and I don't want to break your heart. But my teacher, Mrs. Dara told us we must speak about this *Holodomor*, so people know the horrors that happened. No one talked about it. We need to so that history doesn't repeat itself.

Mrs. Dara wrote this quote on the board, "The Soviet government warned all doctors not to put true cause of death on death certificates. They were told to write a prevalent digestive ailment as the result of death." Can you believe it!

This genocide was not discussed. Journalists were told to shut up. Reporters were blackmailed or paid off not to report about it. Some were warned they could be shot if they reported it. Some Russians, still today, refuse to admit it happened.

Even famous Pulitzer Prize winning journalists like Walter Duranty who was the foreign correspondent for The New York Times lied and wrote, "Russians Hungry, But Not Starving." (Ukrainians were often lumped into being called Russians as Russians wanted total control over Ukraine.)

Mr. Duranty was pro-soviet and convinced President Roosevelt and Americans there was no starvation. Stalin even praised him for his reporting.

Duranty wrote: "There is no actual starvation or deaths from starvation, but there is widespread mortality from disease due to malnutrition...conditions are bad. But there is no famine."

But Duranty didn't really believe what he was writing. We know now that he told the British diplomat William Strang that he reckoned it was "quite possible that as many as 10,000,000 people may have died directly or indirectly from lack of food." That number never appeared in any of Duranty's reporting. It seemed the western world ignored what was going on and believed the Russian government.

The Soviet government hid the famine from people. No one talked about it. At the peak of the famine, in 1933, Stanislav Kosior, who was the Secretary of the Ukrainian Communist Party, wrote a letter to Stalin saying, "any talk of famine should be categorically dismissed."

Did your family talk about hushing up the situation? Did you hear talk like this from the Communist Party? I'm just learning all this information for the first time. It makes no sense to me.

It's a tragic part of Ukrainian history, but it's totally relevant to me as a Ukrainian-Canadian. If you will tell me your story, maybe I can understand.

I feel helpless. Maybe, I can help other atrocities from happening in this world. Mrs. Dara says we need to discuss appalling historical events in class, then teach others.

George Santayana, who won the Nobel prize in literature, said the same thing: "Those who cannot remember the past are condemned to repeat it."

I love you with all my heart, my dearest Dido. You're my flesh and blood and the only Dido I have left. I'd never want to make you sad. But, you're one of the few survivors. I really want you to share your story, as bad and hard as it may be, grandpa.

Love,
Hanusia, your very loving granddaughter

4

September 20

My Dearest, lovely granddaughter, my kalyna,

What are you talking about, my dove? So many questions. Too many questions. You are very persistent, yet I feel if I speak, I may fall ill. You know I would do anything for you. As one of my five precious grandchildren and daughter of Ksenka, I would give you the world. I am so proud of you for wanting to learn. I know how smart you are and that you can easily understand things. But this frightful event is beyond human understanding and borders on insanity.

How can I speak of such real atrocities? Just thinking about it makes me sad.

Later, my sweet. Ask me another day. I cannot tell you now.

I do not feel well. I need to go rest now.

Love,

Dido

5

September 25

My Dearest Dido,

I hope you're feeling better and well rested. I'm writing my paper on the *Holodomor*. It will be part of my final mark in my history class. I don't ever want to cause you distress, but it's just that Mrs. Dara is telling us so many unbelievable things, it's hard to comprehend how this happened and you survived.

For example, in the article Mrs. Dara read to us today, it sounds like Stalin was pure evil! I mean, he killed off more people than Hitler did in the Holocaust! He must have been a psychopath. I'll share some of what I learned today.

The term *Holodomor* refers specifically to the "brutal artificial famine" created by Stalin's regime. It started primarily in ethnically Ukrainian areas in the Northern Caucasus, then spread across parts of Ukraine under Russian control.

This Great Famine was the best kept secret and biggest tool initiated by Stalin. To repress freedom, he used food as a weapon to confiscate land. Ukraine was the third largest exporter of wheat, and was known as the "breadbasket of Europe", said reporter Robert Fulford.

The Ukrainian genocide was purposely enacted to kill Ukrainians who did not submit to the Soviet regime and Communism. It is estimated that one in four Ukrainians were killed intentionally. Stalin engineered it, then bragged to Winston Churchill about his plan. Stalin's henchmen took all the grain, seed, and remaining food they could find from Ukraine's countryside. Villages were abandoned and farmers were evicted from their own land.

This is appalling. I can't believe someone in power can be so cruel and carry on like this without anyone stopping them. I can't imagine what you might have experienced, considering other survivors' stories like this one:

"The dead were all around: on the roads, near the river, by the fences. I used to have five brothers. Altogether 792 people have died in our village during the famine, in the war years – 792 souls."

What happened in your village, grandpa? To you? Please tell me if this is true or if maybe my teacher has it all wrong. I'm hoping she does.

Your caring granddaughter,
Hanusia

6

September 30

My Dearest holubka,

It breaks my heart to tell you what happened to me, but if I do, will you promise to stop pestering me? My heart contains all the memories.

I grew up in the small village of Kosivka, in Odesa Oblast region. There were about 800 people living there and our ancestors had lived there for thousands of years. I can still see my family - my mama, batko, six sestry, and two braty. Their faces, their dying faces, haunt me to this day. It was like walking in the kingdom of death.

In my village, more than 780 people were wiped out. It became a ghost town. Only a few survived by hiding in the bushes. It was horrific. At the start of the famine, the church bells rang when someone died. Later, they sometimes tolled seven times a day. People built wooden coffins at first, said prayers over the dead and buried the bodies. Then, as more died, there were too many bodies for individual funerals and coffins. They just wrapped them in cloth.

No one had the time, or the strength, to bury the dead. In some cases, people who were alive were mistaken as dead, and thrown into the mass grave sites as well. I heard one man say as they threw him on the death wagon, "Wait, I'm not dead." The soldier just laughed and said, "It does not matter, you will be tomorrow."

Bodies were everywhere. We had to burn them. The smell of rotting flesh, sickening. Have you ever smelled burning flesh? I pray you never will.

In the end, the dead were just thrown together in open graves, pits, wastelands, wells, long ditches, gorges, or allotment gardens. No cemeteries, no priests. Too many bodies. No one left to bury the dead. I saw a big pile of logs, a woodpile, or so I thought it was. Then, on walking closer, I realized it was a pile of bodies with their arms and legs sticking out, frozen solid in wintertime from the snow.

For a while, the church bells were continuously sounding. Eventually, though, there was no one left to pull the bells. No one left except a few weak survivors. No one left to say prayers for the dead.

So terrifying. My heart breaks just hearing a church bell to this day. Later, the communist regime took down all the bells in all the villages and had them melted down. They recognized the importance of bells to Ukrainian people as the bells were used in their religious services.

Our neighbour took his three starving children to the city and left them there, hoping someone would feed them or, if possible, they would be helped by a caring family or allowed by the government to stay in the orphanage. There were so many orphans. So much crying and crying and crying. Then the sobbing ceased and tears evaporated into death.

I still have nightmares about the fires. Cannot say anymore now. I need to go out in the fresh air. I still smell those bodies burning and hear those church bells ringing. It was awful.

I remember our last priest saying, "Death was calling like a black shadow."

Dido

7

October 5

My Dearest Dido,

It must have been so terrible for you, a small child, to see, smell, hear, feel. I'm so sorry for what happened to you. I'm so, so, so sorry. What can I do to help you with your bad dreams? I didn't mean to make you sick and relive the horror. I'm very sorry for all your pain and suffering. I didn't know everything that had happened to you. I guess I'm naïve and think what my teacher is telling me is just like fiction. That this could occur to real people and especially my grandfather, whom I love so much is absurd.

If I was there, I would give you a big hug. Please forgive me for asking so many questions. I love you!

In my research for my history paper, I learned that George Simenon, the Belgian novelist who spent a few days in Odesa and observed beggars, was told by the Soviet government officials that the beggars should not be pitied as they simply hadn't adapted to the Communist regime, so "There is nothing for them but to die."

Dido, did you see beggars? Was your family able to help them? Did you have to beg?

We studied the memoirs of one survivor, Eugenia Dallas, who feels that survivors of the Holodomor need to forgive. Is forgiveness possible, Dido? Could you forgive?

Love,
Your granddaughter,
Hanusia Hrabowa

8

October 10

My Dearest Hanusia,

One can never forget such atrocities. The *Holodomor* is embedded in my brain. It haunts my soul. It wants to kill my spirit, but I do not let it. I try not to remember but agree forgiveness is necessary. But not for Stalin!

Forgiveness is the only way. I completely agree with this Eugenia Dallas. We forgive as an act of mercy to heal ourselves. If we do not forgive, we will stay stuck in the past, angry and depressed. This would be like pouring battery acid on yourself.

I forgive because to be fully human I must!

Love
Dido

9

October 15

My Dearest Dido,

My heart bleeds for you. God, what was Stalin thinking? He must have sold his soul to the devil. I'm so, so terribly sorry for everything that happened to you and all those people. I feel so helpless. People use their power to do such evil things.

What can we do, Grandpa, to stop suffering?

Holly Paluck, a *Holodomor* educator said, "Stalin's collectivisation robbed people of much more than food. It was an assault, a systematic cultural, physical and spiritual genocide that attempted to destroy everything, including Ukrainian people's faith and religion." I am using her words in my essay.

Stalin didn't rob us of our culture, did he, Grandpa? We keep our traditions and language. We showed that wicked man a thing or two about Ukrainian people's faith. He didn't defeat us.

Our teacher was also talking about the *kulaks* in class today. Dido, do you have further information about the *kulaks*? So far, I've learned that Stalin branded *kulaks/kurkuls* as "enemies of the people" because they were considered the backbone of the Ukrainian nation and they were proud of their culture and tried to fight back. Stalin figured that by destroying them he could destroy all peasants.

Mrs. Dara says there were a few journalists reporting the facts like American Maurice Hindus. He talked about the *kulaks*, these peasants who rebelled against Russia, saying, "When therefore a man came into possession of two or three horses, as many or a few more cows, about half a dozen pigs, and when he raised three or four hundred *poods* of rye or wheat, he fell into the category of *kulak*."

Stalin wanted to teach the villagers a lesson and on January 7, 1933 (Ukrainian Christmas Day), he wrote, "*Kulak* Ukrainian farmers constitute the driving power of the national movement. We have smashed the *kulaks* and prepared the way for their annihilation." Stalin went on to say that *kulaks* were supposedly the richer peasants and owned more land than others, so they were deported or thrown from their homes. Some that stayed were eventually killed on Stalin's orders.

But these supposedly rich peasants on average only owned about twelve acres, a cow, a horse, ten sheep, a hog and some chickens.

"*Kulaks* would be rounded up, stripped to their underclothes, blackmailed out of their possessions, mocked and humiliated and sometimes shot."

Did this happen to your family members too, Grandpa? I hope not. This is terrifying! I'm learning so much of what took place and understand you know what happened. Grandpa, I really need to discuss this with someone that knows the truth instead of just putting what my teacher tells me in my essay. Was your family considered *kurkuls*, Dido? Is that why your village was almost wiped out?

Love,
Hanusia

10

October 20

My Dearest Dido,

Dido, I know I haven't heard back from you since my last letter a few days ago, but I had to write again. Mrs. Dara showed us a picture of the commemorative pin, designed by Oleh Lesiuk, symbolizing the decree which became known as the law of "Five Ears of Grain." It had five stalks of wheat wrapped up with a thin black ribbon. She said grain was a symbol for the livelihood of many nations and especially to Ukrainians, many of whom were farmers. But during the *Holodomor,* grain was used as a weapon of genocide, to destroy the fabric of Ukrainian people. Bread was more valuable than gold because even if you had gold you could not always buy bread.

When I visit you and Baba, she makes homemade bread. I can't believe she still makes six loaves every week! It's so tasty and I just love to eat it with butter, fresh and hot from the oven. I can't imagine a life without bread in it. Bread is such a vital part of Ukrainian culture. The Ukrainian welcoming dance honours others by sharing and presenting our sacred bread and salt. Ukrainians' strong Christian faith revolves around the importance of bread and salt to our life just like Jesus represents the bread of life and salt of the earth to us.

Baba makes such delicious *kolach*, that braided bread, all the time. It's so yummy!

During the *Holodomor*, there was the penalty of death for holding onto grain. Grandpa, did you hear about this law? Were you shocked when Stalin implemented this law of "Five Stalks of Grain"? My research said that on August 7, 1932 Stalin ordered a death sentence or ten years imprisonment to anyone accused of misappropriation of collective farm property, or *kolhosp*. This law was created to organize further mass arrests and executions. The grain, that was central to Ukrainians for their survival, was confiscated.

What a disturbed man!

Please write to me soon.

Love,
Hanusia

11

October 25

My Dearest Child,

Some days I do not have the strength or will to write to you as all this you are saying is true and yes very dreadful and disturbing.

Our family was considered kurkuls and tried to stand up to the soldiers. I remember it all well; especially when that law came into place. Deaths occurred daily. Simply for eating kernels of grain.

At the beginning of the *Holodomor*, many people revolted and tried to stop Stalin, but the soldiers' weapons spoke louder than our words.

Soon we became hungry and weak. The fight was gone, and people were completely helpless. As a child, at first, I did not really understand the full impact of the law.

As an adult, even now, one still cannot comprehend the magnitude of this so called "death by starvation." At times, I cannot fully wrap my mind around the *Holodomor* and believe what happened.

When remembering, it still feels like an extremely, raw bad nightmare.

Your Dido

12

October 30

My Dearest Dido,

You could not fight back as a child – but grandpa you could fight now for the truth to be known to the entire world! You have defeated Stalin and his regime by sharing your truth. What you are telling me is truly painful. I know you are tired and hurting, body and soul. I love you!

I'm learning so many details from my teacher. I feel a need to write and share what I have learned, and have you verify it. I understand my letters might be too frequent for you to reply. Writing to you is my way of expressing my anger at the situation. I can only imagine what you are experiencing. There are so many questions and there seems no logical answer to the reason Stalin would do this to so many people. It makes no sense to me. I can only imagine what you must have felt as a child.

Grandpa, this new *Holodomor* information makes me feel overwhelmed. I constantly think of those poor, helpless, hungry people.

Ukrainians were kept prisoners in their own villages and couldn't travel to find food or get help. The few people that escaped to cities to work or find food were deemed illegals. People living in the city were told bad things about these peasants and farmers and that they just weren't cooperating with the government.

It is no surprise that Stalin sent 112,000 Bolshevik agents to Ukraine to take property and items he now considered "state-owned", including Ukrainian gold and silver. He wanted it all. Stalin and his Russian army did what they wanted. If they wanted the grain, they took it. If they wanted to arrest someone, they did that as well.

Stalin was trying to take away everything, but he didn't succeed, and you survived, Dido. Your family is here because of your real courage and great strength.

I read that in the fall of 1932, any village that didn't deliver a certain amount of grain was placed on a "blacklist." The army moved in and peasants were condemned to a death sentence. Farmers in the villages who rebelled or could not supply the grain quotas were put on this list. Ukraine became a starvation ghetto. In some villages everyone died. One Ukrainian who travelled from the city to the countryside noted the empty places and said, "The moon was the only remaining witness." It must have been eerie.

Was your village blacklisted, Grandpa?

Your very loving granddaughter,
Hanusia

13

November 5

My Dearest granddaughter,

I remember the day the notice that stated we were blacklisted was posted in Kosivka's village square. A meeting was held, and everyone had to attend and report to village officials to find out how much more grain they had to give. But there was nothing left. No grain anywhere. Nothing hidden or to be found. Not a speck, not a kernel. So many sights, sounds, smells and feelings of despair.

To taste again, to feel again to simply touch another human being. What was left? Starvation. Skin and bones. Hungry bellies. There were people eating parts of corpses to stay alive because there was no food.

There was nothing left to give. The soldiers were not satisfied. They became like devils in our village. Pain and loss - all that was left. Yes, eeriness - and strangeness.

Sorrowful,
Dido

14

November 10

My Dearest Dido,

I must share this with you. Today, I learned Stalin lied to the world and was even cruel to Russians and his own family. My teacher told us that Stalin and the Communists blamed crop failure for people starving to death, but now we know the truth.

Soviet bins were full, and the government exported grain to Germany and other countries. At the height of the *Holodomor*, almost two million tons of grain were put on the market by the Soviets and exported to western nations. The Communist Party set these impossibly high grain quotas for Ukraine to send to Russia. It's completely outrageous that the USSR exported and sold this grain and were starving intentionally. These were human beings at the mercy of the government.

My blood boils when I think of what they did to so many people. It infuriates me, and my heart is full of anger.

Wow. This story is beyond nuts. I was disgusted to read about one man in Ukraine who refused to give his cow to the collective farm during the *Holodomor* and killed it. When the soldiers found out, he was forced to walk around the village with the dead cow's head tied to his neck. I can't believe the Russian government could take away his only cow and then humiliate this farmer in this way. All this is unbelievable, really, Grandpa. I'm so sorry.

Love,
Hanusia

15

November 15

Dearest granddaughter, my little soloveyko,

There are so many things I could respond to in all your letters. I know it is terrifying for you to hear about the *Holodomor* as there are no reasonable explanations that could justify any of Stalin's actions. My life, during that time, though I was a child, was filled with great sorrow.

I lost my mama, Marie, and batko, Ivan. I lost all six of my sestry - Ksenka, Natasia, Mariana, Sofi, Stefanie, and Kaska. And I lost my two braty, Petro and Vasyl. They died before my eyes. We were a happy family, not much money but rich in kindness. We worked hard making a living farming, growing our own big gardens and raising our livestock. We always had enough to eat with a few cows, chickens and pigs. We were rarely sick.

Then, in 1929, the state-owned Communists' collective farms came. The government took away all private ownership of land from the farmers. Everyone was expected to farm and work together. The Comrade was the main boss, and when soldiers came into the villages everything changed instantly. They deemed us kulaks just because we owned our land.

They demanded we sign over our farms and if we didn't, they said we were "enemies of the state," and then just took the farms from us. It was all done in the name of communism or collectivisation, so the state or the USSR could own everything and take away Ukraine's independence.

My family, friends and neighbours, all of us, went from having enough to having nothing, from health to malnutrition. Bellies swelling from hunger, skin and bones in the course of one year. Grandfathers were begging for bread on the streets to feed their grandchildren. There was widespread disease – cholera, typhus, scurvy, pneumonia, diphtheria, tuberculosis, and skin conditions.

There were very unsanitary conditions from so many dead bodies left lying around, which led to unclean drinking water and no place to wash properly.

Many Ukrainians deemed uncooperative were shipped away by trains to Siberia, killed or made to work for the collective farms. Any resistance, and you were shot on the spot. No one invited them into our villages, but the Soviet brigades came by force with guns to confiscate our land, food and wheat. They mocked our faith and sent our priests away. They closed our churches or used them for government meetings. The church was the centre of our faith in the village and all activities stemmed from the heart of the church. They stole or destroyed our icons and hung up pictures of Stalin. The Soviets declared, "God is not here. We are greater than God. We stomp on God." We had to hold our religious practices in secret.

We had to attend daily meetings about "collectivisation." They told us not to believe in God and banned traditional holidays like Christmas and Easter and the saints' days.

All was lost. Our daily lives changed - no christenings, no weddings, no funerals, no music. Music - a huge part of our culture - was just gone.

After a while, we were not allowed to leave our villages to search for food. They simply starved us to death. We were totally controlled by Stalin's strong, armed men. In daily meetings, we were told to be thankful, all this is for the good of the party, we should be grateful to the government. They gave no sympathy. Stalin's goal was to bring Ukraine to its knees. He was terrified of losing Ukraine and he wanted to stop any Ukrainian nationalistic activity.

Villages were placed on blacklists. People were deported and arrested, travel bans were put in place and borders were closed. Stalin also demanded loan payments for wheat and taxes on land. Soldiers came back again and again on orders from Stalin to search for food. Nothing was left. I was the smallest and I would sneak away to the bushes to try and find us something to eat.

How did I survive? Bozhe! Perhaps that is why I am called Bohdan, "gift from God." I survived by the grace of God and my lovely mama. I found out later that she was giving me her portion of food, the last of the kolach and the pulp from the sugar beets. She died and I lived because of her great sacrifice. However, at times, I would have preferred to die with my family and not be left an orphan, all alone and having to relive this terror.

Indifference and apathy were everywhere. It destroyed our relationships, families, and villages. Death became a desirable relief. We believed death was our only escape from this hell.

My neighbour Vasyl told me, "People didn't look like people – they were more like starving ghosts. My mother looked like a glass jar, filled with clear spring water. All her body that could be seen...was see-through and filled with water, like a plastic bag."

Although we were alive, our lives were gone. People were fearful and suspicious of each other. Paranoia was rampant. We were lost, without hope and assistance. Famine was a silent killer, like a snake slithering into our souls. It had destroyed us completely, taking away our dignity, compassion and love for each other.

I was young like you once. But I had no childhood. It was a very dark time. I escaped a terrible death but lived. I am so glad I came to Canada and you did not have to experience what happened to me. I am very grateful for the opportunity to have had a family and have you, my beautiful granddaughter, in my life. These memories are in the past and should stay hidden in the darkness.

Love,
Grandfather

16

November 18

My Dearest Dido,

Your survival and tenacity grandfather really make me believe in the power of God! These vicious acts by the Soviet government as you mention and, in my essay, demonstrate clearly their mandate and fearful nature. For example: the main Administrator for the Soviet government, Lazar Kaganovich was corrupt and hateful by taking all the grain and killing innocent people. Stalin and he went after the parts of Ukraine that had the most desired resources. They wanted and took it all: wheat, coal, copper, flax, mercury, zirconium, and zinc.

In 1929, in the name of communism, any educated Ukrainians were labelled a *kulak*, and artists and poets promoting Ukrainian ideas were deemed dangerous. Some reports tell us that 1,000,000 Ukrainian peasants who wouldn't willingly give up their land were considered a threat to the government.

These people were killed or deported. It's all very scary. Stalin was determined to squash all Ukrainian independence at any cost.

Love forever,
Hanusia

17

November 20

Dear little babushka,

As an adult, I have since learned the *Holodomor* was a deliberate act to eliminate a nation. It was all staged and planned out by Stalin. He bragged about being a leader, teacher and father but now we know the ugly truth.

The *Holodomor* was an act of genocide against the Ukrainian people committed by the Soviet Communist regime. They wanted our land, our homes, our everything. They tried to break our spirits and even take our souls. We were innocent victims. They wanted to "Russify" Ukrainians and take away our culture so we had no roots.

Stalin tried to destroy our economic structure as well as our customs and morals. Our land, jobs, industries, food, freedom, and religious practices were taken from us. The Soviet government forbade the Ukrainian language and put a stop to cultural activities to create suffering.

Ukraine had an enormous amount of resources and very fertile land. Even during the Second World War, Hitler took over a part of Ukraine and brought large trucks to steal Ukraine's good, black soil and haul truckloads of it back to Germany.

Youth brigades were trained in support of the Stalin regime. They lived off the land and ate whatever they confiscated from the peasants. They committed cruel and humiliating acts against the peasants like forcing them to fight for sport or crawl and bark like dogs. These youth brigades even raped women.

Extreme measures were done by government soldiers like spreading poison over potatoes, grain, and any remaining plants that could be used for food. People were encouraged to report on others who were hiding food. Before the Russian invasion, the farmers were free. Joseph Stalin did not want us to assimilate with Russia, but rather to wipe us off the face of the earth.

The Soviet army tried to eliminate Ukrainians, so they could take our homes and confiscate our possessions. They were trying to fill the vacant villages with villagers from Russia. Soldiers came, broke windows and doors, took our linen and kicked us out of our homes. Anyone that did not cooperate was said to have "difficulties in transition." When we asked, "Where should we go?", the soldiers would tell us in cold blood, "There is no place on Earth for you, so die."

We had to sleep outside as we were kicked out of homes, unbearable in winter as it was freezing temperatures. We nearly froze to death. It was an abnormally bitter cold winter in 1933, sometimes -20C or colder. When Ukrainians fought back, their houses were burned to the ground or they were tortured, imprisoned and finally killed.

At first, the educated priests and artists were arrested, then deported to foreign lands - 250 poets and scholars just gone. They were considered our leaders and Stalin believed they promoted Ukrainian nationalism. If he got rid of the educated, he felt, he could control the peasants.

The kulaks' spirit of independence had to be broken. Over a period of four years, they were banished to concentration camps like the Gulag, terrorized, arrested, executed, or they just disappeared. The soldiers were cruel and ruthless and wanted to hammer nails in our coffins.

It was an inconceivable period in the history of Ukrainian people. My dreams are haunted with sickness, starvation and death. I have only bitter childhood memories.

My family - my greatest irreplaceable love - was taken from me. Material possessions can be replaced but my entire family died, starved to death before my eyes.

I am constantly tormented by their faces, and their images are embedded on my heart. I was numb and could not even shed a tear, my emotions shrivelled like my body. I saw dead bodies in my dreams and cried in my sleep.

My clothes were ragged, and I had bare feet. I remember continually visualizing Zenny, our neighbour. The last time we saw her before she starved to death, Taras, my best friend remarked that she looked more like a shadow than a human being.

I remember a strange silence everywhere. Nobody cried, moaned, or complained. Death was at our door. I felt it was the end. Ukrainian villages were in decay, empty, deserted and miserable.

I have heard that a starving person is simply too weak to fight back. Hunger overwhelms even the urge to object. Many people suffered from hallucinations, psychosis, depression because of hunger. Their legs and bellies became swollen as the body retained water.

Some people tried to escape through the Polish border by crossing the Zbruch River, the border between Poland and Ukraine, but Stalin closed and sealed that border and Ukrainians were gunned down or drowned when trying to escape across it.

I must go now. My tears flow constantly, just like where the Opir and Stryi Rivers meet in western Ukraine.

Did you know that these rivers are known as "the rivers of blood"?

Love,
Your tormented Dido

18

November 22

My Dearest Dido,

In August 1932, Stalin's niece, Kira Alliluyeva, visited Kyiv and told Stalin's wife to tell Stalin she saw people starving, begging, thin, with swollen bellies and distorted eyes at the train station. But Stalin refused to acknowledge the famine, brushing aside her comments. "She's a child, she makes things up." She was 13 at the time, only a little younger than me.

Stalin rarely listened to advisors and exterminated any perceived enemies. His own wife, Nadezhda Alliluyeva, apparently committed suicide on November 9, 1932, but her death certificate just said she had an open wound to the heart. I bet she had a wound to the heart living with that heartless man!

Heartless, heartless, heartless! His own wife. Stalin was the biggest manipulator and deceiver in the world. He showed no remorse. A pure evil creature!

Stalin turned a blind eye to starving people. He justified any factual reports. Another example, Arthur Koestler, a British author and journalist, then in Kharkiv, described these events: "The stations were lined with begging peasants with swollen hands and feet, the women holding up to the carriage windows horrible infants with enormous wobbling heads, stick-like limbs and swollen pointed bellies...They returned to die in the villages."

Those poor starving people. Why didn't anyone help them? I can't image seeing that trauma. I'm torn up inside. It's enough to give you nightmares. The soldiers were totally in charge and the peasants weren't allowed to make decisions themselves or have any rights.

Love,
Hanusia

19

November 25

My Dearest Dido,

You know I love you dearly. We've always been close. I would never knowingly harm you. I've just been trying to understand what happened and how it occurred, and when I heard you lived and survived this *Holodomor*, I just had to know the facts. And I thank you for sharing your difficult life story. I understand it's very upsetting to write letters about the *Holodomor* to me.

I'd never heard about this genocide before my teacher told us about it. Many Ukrainians are just learning about the *Holodomor*. It's now part of the high school curriculum, and of course it should be taught. But knowing there are people in the world, in Canada, that survived and are living today to share their stories is hard to imagine. It's hard to wrap my head around it.

But facts are facts, and there were eyewitness accounts stating, "millions of people are wandering naked, starving in the woods, stations, towns and farms begging for a piece of bread." One quote I read says, "only Ukraine was starving." One girl cried, "Only Ukraine was honoured with this crown of thorns."

I love you deeply.

Love,
Hanusia

20

November 30

Dear precious granddaughter,

I still believe good prevails over evil. But sometimes I wonder, especially when I see so many bad things happening in the world still today, with wars and refugees and famines.

Death, to me, may one day be good news. A person, the human spirit and body, can only take so much turmoil. What can we do? Pray, pray always, always pray.

Oye Bozhe!

Be kind and try and help where you can. A very simple philosophy.

We are born to die. What is our purpose here? Philosophers and others, more knowledgeable than me, have tried to answer age-old questions. Answers to why, why, why?

Saint Mother Teresa of Calcutta says, "It is not the big things we do in life that are important but the little things, done with love." She dedicated her life to the poor in India. That is what I have learned and try to do – "small things with great love".

Be content with what you have and try to find and promote peace. Be kind! It is important that young people, all people, remember and do not forget.

I remember an old Ukrainian proverb: "Bread is everyone's master." They took every kernel of grain. The harvest and even the seed reserves. We even tried to eat the stalks of the grain; we were so hungry. The soldiers would dig in the gardens and ground with steel rods trying to find our hidden food. A mother in our village had a bundle of corn hidden in her apron and they found it, pushed her to the ground and took it. She was just flung down, stepped on and lay weeping. The soldiers had lost their hearts.

Another family thought they could outsmart the soldiers and built a double wall in their house to hide food behind, but the soldiers found it and kicked the father to death and then sent the rest of the entire family away to Siberia on the Red Train. This was another form of punishment the Russian government used on people that were uncooperative or would not accept communism and collective farms.

All the animals were taken or shot - horses, cows, calves and sheep. Some tried to hide their cow. My mother, Marie, begged the soldier not to kill our only animal so we could have milk to feed my baby brother. My mother could not nurse him, as her milk was all dried up. But the soldier just laughed and shot it dead right in front of my mother and all of us. My mama fell crying to the ground, sobbing her heart out, knowing the grave consequences of losing her last source of food. Those that had hid their cow could have milk and were more likely to survive the famine.

Our neighbour lady, Sophie, had a shawl and a pair of boots and the soldiers demanded them. When she refused, they pushed her down and took them from her.

City workers would bring wagons and fill them full of our household items, and then take them to sell in the city at Russian-controlled stores called Torgsins. The stores were a front by the Russian government to take the last of our gold, silver or anything valuable in trade for bits of food. These stores had an abundance of goods on display for sale, so the foreign press could report Ukrainians had access to goods. But we had nothing left to trade, as armed men had confiscated all our wares. It was a dog eat dog world, as no one was to be trusted.

My neighbours wrote pleading letters to their relatives abroad for food packages as supplies were much needed as there was nothing to eat.

And everyone was silent. We were not allowed to talk about what was happening or that we were hungry. At schools and homes, places were quiet. We could not mention the dead or grieve for our family members. It was strictly forbidden. Keep your mouth shut or be arrested. Silence was Stalin's greatest tool.

We were scared to talk. Fear, our constant companion. Finally, too weak to talk.

After my family died, my friend Taras and I ate whatever we could find in the alleys or the woods. I know you have pets and I am embarrassed to say we ate dogs and cats. We also ate rats, mice, boiled frogs and toads, crows, pigeons, sparrows, roots, tree bark, buds from linden trees, leaves, grass, moss, marigolds, and bits of corn, hemp seeds, flowers, dandelions, thistles, caterpillars and quail eggs, and if the hospital threw out peels, we ate them too.

We ate anything we could stomach and get our hands on, even slurping pig slop from a common cauldron. Potatoes, milled acorn, horseradish scraps, pigweed, rabbits, squirrels and any burrowing animal. Some people even ate mator zhenyko with no flour, just a mixture of weeds and crushed straw made into patties.

If a horse dropped dead, it was burned to try and get rid of disease and then cooked and eaten later. However, many people then became infected with glanders disease, an infectious disease that is caused by the bacteria when eating dead horses.

If we tried to eat the wheat stalks on the fields, we were shot. One of the last items Taras and I ate before leaving Ukraine was a porcupine. And as I ate, I imagined the scent of delicious food.

Survivors had huge swollen bellies, but we were so hungry. Our arms and legs looked like scary skeletons, our skin translucent over hallowed faces, our eyes bulging and crazed from terror. We looked like corpses and death was desirable. I felt we were "artificial orphans" as this starvation was purposely caused by Stalin in the name of universal collectivisation. The world seemed indifferent to this disaster.

During Remembrance Day, governments around the world use the red poppy to symbolize loss, but the black flag was flown in Ukraine during the *Holodomor*.

I still feel helpless and sick talking about it. Pray for me, my sweet child.

Love from your long suffering,
Grandpa Bohdan

21

December 5

Dear Dido,

I pray for you every day, Dido, and all the victims of the *Holodomor*. Studying this has made me aware of how grateful I am to live in Canada, a free country, but also to have had great parents and grandparents like you and Baba in my life. It gives me hope upon hearing your sad story.

Just yesterday, for my report, I read in Anne Applebaum's book, Red Famine, that for some families, keeping a cow was literally a matter of life and death.

The part about the cow sticks in my mind since I was so fond of Bessy, our brown dairy cow. I even tried to milk her a few times when I came to visit you each summer, but that never worked out. I never thought of how important cows and grain are to life, but hearing your story makes me think differently.

How are you? I know I'm causing you great pain reliving this horror. I didn't know the full extent of what really happened to you, your family members, and Ukrainians, during all this destruction, starvation and evil. I wish I could be there right now with you to give you a gigantic hug. I feel your sorrow deeply. What can I do to help you, grandpa? I will continue to pray for you daily.

Love,
Hanusia

22

December 10

Dear granddaughter, my sertse,

One can never be truly well after going through this experience. One survives but is never really the same. Experiencing war, torture, starvation, death, genocide – *Holodomor* changes you. My heart carries memories that will never be erased. I live and have lived only for my children and grandchildren. There are things I have seen that leaves a person in trauma.

In my village, we eventually had nothing to eat, and there were secret police and informants everywhere. We could not trust anyone. We would go looking for grain and sugar beets. There was a foul vinegar smell in the air from all the corpses and burning of homes in the village. I was walking one day and saw a wagon of corpses and a quarry full of bodies. The man that picked up corpses received half a pound of bread per dead body.

There were no burial services, no prayers, no divine liturgy, no Panakhyda (funeral liturgies) nor Parasta (prayers of the dead), or even time to mourn. There was no one left to even moan. It was a silent sorrow that filled the earth. I felt like I was in hell. My family, all dead. Ukraine had become a country of graves, crosses and death - no doctors, teachers, and priests. Why should I go on?

Taras and I had to sleep wherever we could. They threw us out of our homes, so we hid in haystacks. Hanna Doroshenko, a survivor from our village, called this a "bloodless war." This term is mentioned in the Bible. It is when innocent people die.

Your grandfather,
Grandpa Bohdan

P.S. Please, no more questions!

23

December 15

Dear Dido,

This is unthinkable! I can't understand the workings of nasty people. How did this happen? How could it have happened? How did you get out Dido? How did you come to Canada? What happened to you?

I wish I was with you now.

Love,
Hanusia

24

January 14

Dear Dido,

Why have you quit writing to me? Are you mad at me? I promise, no more questions. I was wrong to bug you. Please just write to me!

Love,
Your granddaughter,
Hanusia

25

January 16

Dear Dido,

My mother says you're sick and that's why you haven't written. I'm sorry I bothered you with so many questions. Those memories made you sick. Please forgive me. I was wrong. Please get better soon.

Love,
Hanusia

P.S. I love you so much!

26

January 17

Dear Diary,

My Dido's not writing to me anymore. I'm worried about him.

I finished my essay. I included all the parts I wrote to Grandpa about in my essay as well as the information that he had shared. Mrs. Dara said it was excellent. I want to share this news with him.

Peace,
H.

27

January 18

Dear Diary,

My precious Dido was taken to the hospital in an ambulance. He has a very high fever and is now in a coma. My mother and I are going to see him in the hospital. I feel awful. I caused this to happen to my special grandfather because of my probing. Why did I pester him? I bugged him so much, just because I had so many questions. I feel terrible.

Peace,
H.

28

January 19

Dear Diary,

Mom's allowing me to miss school and stay by his bedside. She gets that I feel responsible but assures me it's not my fault. I'm not leaving grandfather's side till he's better. I'll sit by his bed, put a warm cloth on his forehead and hold his hand till he's well. Grandpa's having terrible nightmares and cold sweats. He keeps shouting and crying in his sleep. He's sobbing through his dreams. I feel terrible.

Peace,
H.

29

January 20

Dear Diary,

I can't stop crying. I don't even want to go to school. I feel horrible. I brought this on him, pushing him and prodding him to tell his story. I kept bothering him about all those awful things. Why was I so stubborn and nosey? This isn't a history lesson. This is life. My life and my Dido's life. I love Dido with all my heart and soul, and I don't want him to be sick.

Peace,
H.

30

January 21

Dear Diary,

What if he dies because of me? I feel dreadful, awful and full of grief. I need to get down on my knees and pray. Perhaps by writing my prayer on paper it becomes a stronger request and God will answer it.

God, please forgive me for hurting my grandpa. Help him heal and get better and I promise never to question him again about the past, the Holodomor or anything. I promise with all my heart and soul. Help me, dear God, and make Grandpa well.

Peace,
H.

31

January 24

Dear Diary,

Grandpa's still in a coma and has been for the past week. Every day I arrive early at the hospital and stay until the nurses kick me out of his room at night to go home to bed. When I'm with grandpa, I keep talking to him. I tell him how much I love him and how sorry I am for being so demanding.

Peace,
H.

32

January 25

Dear Diary,

Finally, after eight days, Dido's fever broke. I was still at the hospital, sleeping in a chair. I woke up to a weak voice. "Water, please, water, a sip of water, dyakuyu, thanks."

It was Grandpa. I quickly jumped up and gave him a glass of water.

"Are you okay, Grandpa? I'm so sorry, please forgive me." I started to cry. "I don't want to lose you. I shouldn't have asked all those questions. I'll stop now. Sorry, sorry, sorry! No more letters. I promise. No more questions. I'll never bother you about the Holodomor again. I promise. Just get better, Dido."

He said, "My darling granddaughter Hanusia, I need to sleep now to get better, but when I awaken, we will talk."

Peace,
H.

33

January 28

Dear Diary,

Grandpa slept for three days straight, and now that his fever's gone, he's started eating again. Yesssss! Feeling stronger, he finally spoke to me, quietly at first, then with a passion and urgency like I'd never seen before.

"My dove," Dido said, "the Holodomor is the past. What is done is done. However, it is important to remember the past, even though the past does not define us. You are right. I need to talk about the atrocities. It is essential I speak up now, even if it leads to my death. Ukrainians cannot be silent anymore."

"Grampa, please do not speak now as you need to rest and get better," I said.

Peace,
H.

34

February 27

Dear Diary,

When Dido got home, it was like he was on a mission. He shared what happened to him, his family, his friends and Ukrainians. I received this beautiful handwritten letter from him. I've glued it here in my diary as I don't want to lose it.

Peace,
H.

35

February 27

Dear Hanusia,

As promised, I will reveal all I remember about the *Holodomor*. I am writing this letter to tell you how I escaped. After my family died, I did not want to live. However, my friend Taras constantly encouraged me to keep going. He pulled me along and never gave up. Without his friendship and strength, I would have died.

We were living in the woods. It is there we met up with another small group of young orphans. We had no one to return to in our village.

A red wagon came to villages to pick up the orphans and take them by train to Russian orphanages. Ukraine was now fully occupied and controlled by the Communist Russians. The government wanted to take surviving children to train them to serve in the Russian army, support collectivism and its propaganda. We were called "Little Stalin's Children." Stalin tried to indoctrinate the *Holodomor* survivors, especially the children, by having them shout, "Long live the Communist Party and long live the Soviet regime." His slogan was, "He who does not work does not eat."

We knew we had to get out of there somehow. It was Taras' idea to cross over to Poland. He was so courageous. I was terrified the whole journey. But he kept his arm around my shoulder to comfort me the entire trip. Together, as we were so small, we were able to hide in a wooden box on the train and escape across the border to Poland. Taras and I were taken to an orphanage where we were able to go to school.

Tragically, soon after, Taras succumbed to typhoid and died. It was an extremely sad day for me. I felt utterly alone. I was devastated. He was like my brother. Without his persistent help and encouragement, I would not have made it. He saved me. I knew I had to live for both of us, in his memory.

As my mother would say when someone dies, "Vichnaya pamiat!" which means "Memory eternal!"

Later, at the orphanage, when I was 10, I met your beautiful grandmother and we became inseparable friends. We both worked hard to finish our schooling. We married first and had an opportunity to immigrate to Canada in 1954, at the age of 30. The rest you know.

My friend Taras' words of encouragement helped me to move on when I wanted to give up and die. He was named after the great Ukrainian literary hero Taras Shevchenko.

As I think about telling my story, I am reminded of Shevchenko's words as well. He spoke up for injustices for all people and it cost him his freedom and eventually his life. He spoke about freedom, peace and Ukrainian struggles in his Zapovit, or "Testament." People still read and recite Taras' works today. He is considered the "Great Bard of Ukraine."

I knew that these were difficult circumstances, but Shevchenko had not given up, so I needed to follow his example. He struggled, suffered, and died in a Russian prison. I must not give up. I must have the courage to tell anyone who will listen about what happened during the *Holodomor* and share the truth with the rest of the world.

My parents, my two brothers and six sisters, all the people in my village, those millions of voices that lost their lives, those brave souls that tried to stand up against Stalin and fight against his plan of starvation - they are crying from the heavens.

I survived and am here today to share my story, a very difficult and sad, but true, story. I do still believe, good will prevail over evil, but only if we are willing to take risks by standing up against the devil. We need to speak for the dead, be their voices and continually cry out for their justice.

You are correct, my little dove. I survived, and because I did, I had a family - a wife called Jennie and four beautiful children, Petro, your mother Ksenka, Natasia and Mariana, two grandsons, Vasyl and Stefan, and three lovely granddaughters, Sofi, Kaska and you, Hanusia. All of you were named in memory of my family that perished. The *Holodomor* survivors have courageously spoken to the world, "Bread could have saved us then...Remembrance will save us now!"

Let the *Holodomor* be remembered forever. Speak, remember. Like other holocausts, genocides and wars that occurred and are still happening. We need to speak against all injustices against so many people in the world.

Ukrainian people's story of genocide, the *Holodomor*, did truly occur. I am a survivor of this genocide. The number of remaining survivors, though few, must loudly tell their stories and the truth. Using famine,

Stalin bragged about trying to whip Ukrainians into submission and silence. Ukrainians are not lambs to be slaughtered! We are humans with a unique voice.

Some survived to remember, to speak, lest we forget. Our voices ring out like church bells singing, reminding us that we count, we matter, and we exist! We are heard! The devastation was great. Twenty-five percent of the Ukrainian population was eradicated by famine. But some people prevailed. We will forge on against greed, hatred and injustice.

Malcolm Muggeridge, a British journalist for the Manchester Guardian, was one of the lone reporters who told about the horrors. He told the truth even though, at the time, the world turned a blind eye and many reports said there was no famine.

Truth will prevail!

I am here to say the *Holodomor* did happen. I witnessed, survived and give testament to these facts. I, Bohdan, speak for my fellow Ukrainians in the Donetsk area, near the Azov Sea, in my village of Kosivka. I speak for the dead from the many areas across Ukraine affected by this brutal slaughter of innocents. Many brave Ukrainian souls tried to speak but were killed and families were persecuted or arrested and accused of being spies.

As God is my witness, I survived! Finally, I have the strength to speak the truth and tell my story. I am no longer afraid of the past and will never be quiet again. This tragedy, the *Holodomor*, occurred simply because we were Ukrainians.

Stalin wanted to violate, confiscate all private property, and deny all that belonged to Ukrainians in the name of collectivisation. Those that resisted were killed, imprisoned or died by the most terrible means, death by starvation.

Let the healing begin, Hanusia, my love. Please keep writing and come visit me soon. Your Dido needs gigantic hugs so love can prevail. My brightly burning candle will not be quenched. A beacon of light glows for millions of Ukrainian flames that will never be extinguished, if we remember!

Love,
Dido

36

July 1

Dear Diary,

Wow, that was quite the letter from Dido. I haven't written in my diary for quite a while as so much is going on in my life with thoughts about Grandpa, school, and exams.

I'm so happy. His powerful words made me feel energized. I can hardly wait to see him. I feel way better.

It's summer! I'm so excited to go visit Grandpa now during my school holidays. My mom suggested I spend the entire holidays with my grandparents. I'm so pumped to see them both, but especially my grandpa. I need to hang out and have some fun time with Dido. It'll be awesome.

Peace,
H.

37

July 2

Dear Diary,

Now that I have more time and feel better, I would like to share information about my grandparents' village as I soon will be visiting there. Hafford, Saskatchewan is a small village, but it has an interesting history. It's about a one-hour drive away from Saskatoon, 96 kilometres. There is about 360 people living there, so not a huge place, but it's a fun Ukrainian place. Even the street signs are written in the Cyrillic alphabet. Many Ukrainians settled in this area during the first wave of immigration in 1891.

See, I did learn some titbits in my history class. Aren't you impressed, dear diary?

It's so cool my grandma and grandpa live in town, but they have a huge yard and garden on the outskirts of this village. I can ride my bike without worrying about traffic.

Peace,

H.

38

July 3

Dear Diary,

Finally arrived. Grandpa and I spend our first few days weeding the garden, resting in the sunshine, watching the sunflowers bloom like smiling faces and enjoying Dido's beautiful flowers. Grandpa loves growing things and seeing things blossom.

We play cards together, Kaiser and Rummy, and hang out with my Baba too. They let me win most of the time. We cook together and pinch varenyky, or perogies. It's a lot of work but the eating is so good. To make plum perogies, we cut a plum in half, take the seed out and put one half in the rolled-out dough and then close it or pinch the dough together. Then we add the perogies to boiling water, cook, drain, and add butter and top with sour cream. Delicious!! I ate so many my stomach hurt.

We also drink chai with a lot of sugar and milk, just the way I like it. They spoil me and make all my fave foods. I like hearing Grandpa read from Kobzar, Shevchenko's book of poetry. It sounds so haunting at times. I don't know all the Ukrainian words, but Gramps explains when I don't understand.

I feel happy to be here with both grandparents. Some of my friends don't have any grandparents alive. Baba and Dido truly still love each other and are so content together. I hope I find someone that loves me like they do.

Peace,

H

39

July 10

Dear Diary,

Today, Grandpa and I giggled so hard at his funny stories about my mother as a little girl. She was stubborn, just like me. We joked together. It feels so good to laugh. We even spent time practicing my Ukrainian and writing the thirty-three Cyrillic letters of the Ukrainian alphabet.

"Do not forget where you came from, your heritage and traditions. Treasure your ancestors and your culture, as it is your backbone and makes you who you are today." Grandpa reminded me, "You can pick your friends but not your relatives, so treasure them."

Peace,
H.

40

July 30

Dear Diary,

Today, we drove around the countryside. Grandpa let me drive. I enjoyed seeing the magnificent crops and the wheat blooming. Once a farmer, always a farmer, and grandpa loved seeing the wheat heads bowing low, almost ready for harvest.

In the afternoon, he slept in the sunshine in his reclining chair. I held his hand. When he had a bad dream, I wiped his forehead. Grandfather's getting stronger every day. His mind is still sharp as a tack. His body and soul are healing. I'm over the moon and glad Dido is way better.

Peace,
H.

41

August 25

Dear Diary,

Today's my last day with my grandparents. Summer has flown by and I was having so much fun I did not even write in my diary. Sad to go back to Saskatoon. Leaving on a high note, because grandpa's heart is better.

We're both tanned, strong and ready to face anything. Our bond is special and thick as glue. I hate to leave Dido, but back to school. Last year for me, Grade 12. Uggh! Can you believe it! Gotta study hard and get my marks up for university entrance.

"Use that smart mind of yours for good," grandpa said as he hugged me close. "You can become or do anything you want if you study hard."

Education is vital in our family and it was expected upon high school graduation that I attend a post-secondary school and obtain a trade or degree of my choice. So, grandpa's comments were taken seriously.

There were tears of love in both our eyes as we hugged goodbye.

As I drove back home, I knew all was forgiven.

Peace,
H.

42

November 11

Dear Diary,

I got a lovely package from my dearest Dido. Two tickets to Ukraine. Are you serious?!

Wait till my friends hear I'm going to Ukraine. They're going to be so excited for me! I get to miss school as well. My grandfather has not been back to Ukraine since he escaped to Poland during the Holodomor.

This could be scary for him.

It's my eighteenth birthday too! Yassssss. My friends and I are going to a concert to celebrate. I'm so ecstatic! Sorry for not writing but grade 12 is such a busy year.

Peace,

H.

P.S. I taped in Grandpa's letter for you, diary.

43

November 9

Dear granddaughter,

You have awakened a desire to visit the past and confront my demons head on. I feel physically stronger today. With God's help and your assistance, I want to go back to my village Kosivka. After that, I want to visit the capital of Ukraine, Kyiv, to see the *Holodomor* statue erected in remembrance of the millions of people who died of starvation. Among them, my loving family, whom I miss dearly.

This will not be an easy journey, but it is a necessary one. I need to bring closure to this devasting part of my life. It is a wound that will never heal. The scars will always be there, however, my soul requires me to go to Ukraine to see, remember and move forward.

I feel strongly that you need to accompany me on this healing journey, as you have shown great courage and strength to try and understand this genocide. Young people like you are the future and need to see, understand and help prevent such horrors. Education, caring, justice and wisdom will defeat evil. So together, let us trace the difficult steps of my past.

On November 28th, 2006 the Ukrainian parliament recognized the Ukraine famine of 1932-1933 as an act of genocide against the Ukrainian people. The President of Ukraine declared November 26th, 1998 as a national day of remembrance for the victims of this mass atrocity. It is now remembered in Ukraine on the fourth Saturday in November, just like in Canada. I would like to leave soon and be in Kyiv in time for this day, now known as Ukrainian Famine and Genocide Day *Holodomor* Memorial Day.

During this memorial, Ukrainians light candles and say prayers in remembrance of the *Holodomor* and the dead.

Will you come with me?

Always,
Your loving grandfather

44

November 12

Dear Diary,

Still reeling from partying with friends last night. Great show. I can't believe I'm legally an adult and going to Ukraine.

That letter from Dido made my heart leap into my throat. Thinking about the trip today, I'm apprehensive and yes, honestly terrified. Thankfully, my parents are coming too. They knew about my grandfather's plan and discussed this prior to him sending the tickets. Mom said I'd started something and now needed to finish it.

I'm gonna go freak out a bit now.

Peace (or not),
H.

45

November 19

Dear Diary,

Packing for this experience, thinking it's a great adventure, but my heart knows better. Sure, I've never been to Ukraine or flown across an ocean. That part is cool. But it's not like this is a trip to Disneyworld.

What have I got myself into? Yes, it's an important necessary step for our family and, more importantly, Dido. But I can't help but feel I've opened a can of worms and those worms are not slithering away easily once free.

Peace,
H.

46

November 20

Dear Diary,

It was -15C today when the five of us left for the airport. We fly first to Toronto and then on to Kyiv. Luckily, it's warmer in Ukraine, only -5C. I've got a coldness in my hands and in my heart because I worry how grandpa will handle the trip. I hope he doesn't get sick again.

How will he react in Ukraine? What might happen? I'm nervous.

I held my grandfather's hand, waiting for our luggage. His hands were cold too. We both knew what we were up against. Maybe we can get through this together.

Good thing my grandpa's Ukrainian is great. My parents', and especially mine, really sucks. It's way easier to get around when you speak Ukrainian. Dido got us a cab to take us to the Hotel Myr. In two days, we'll travel to Kosivka, the once abandoned village of the dead, the ghost town. No idea what'll happen there. I'm terrified!

Peace,

H.

47

November 21

Dear Diary,

Spent the first day relaxing, walking and hardly eating. Not very hungry. To keep our spirits up, prayers are said often. This is not a tourist visit.

I spend as much time as I can with grandpa. We're inseparable, united by my curiosity and compassion and his desire to finally share his horrific story. Unwilling at first, now he's telling all. Yes, of course, the elephant is in the room. Hopefully, after today, that elephant will be quashed for good.

My grandfather started reminiscing about his short time with his parents, brothers and sisters, and even shared a few funny stories like his mother's catchphrase, "the way you make your bed is the way you will sleep in it."

I chuckled at that because my mother says that to me all the time too. Funny sayings are often carried on in families just like genetics.

Peace,
H.

48

November 22

Finally, big day here. Our guide came early with his van to take us to the countryside. It's a day-long journey, roughly seven and a half hours one way from Kyiv. At times, the roads were mainly dirt roads and there aren't many road signs in the countryside, but the guide knew the way.

We stopped half-way to eat our picnic lunch and met many farmers, Didos and Babas selling vegetables, fruit and flowers on the side of the road.

Martin, our guide explained about modern Ukraine and its continuous fight for freedom. From my history class, I remember Ukraine achieved independence on August 24th, 1991. However, it still has an ongoing fight to be independent as the Russian government has invaded the Crimea area.

Luckily, Ukrainians grow bountiful gardens and food is in abundance now. How ironic is that! Ukraine, once again the breadbasket of Europe.

Still, lots of corruption, and war in the east with Russia's invasion. Ukrainian living wage is very low. A teacher makes the equivalent of about fifty dollars a month.

I sat next to grandfather the entire journey and held his hand. Surprisingly, he's very strong and we drew strength from each other. Soon, too soon, we were there. What did we see? Still a ghost town. When the Russian people came and took over this village, only a few people stayed. About 260 people live here now.

Dido showed us where his home was and recounted another horrible story. He had a neighbour called Yuri. Yuri was put in charge of fetching grain from individual households. When the soldiers came to each village, they'd often put a villager in charge of filling the grain quota. The villagers didn't want to do this but were forced to go to each house and collect grain. Imagine, taking the last morsels of wheat from your hungry friends and family members. And still sadder yet, if the village didn't meet the monthly grain quota, the grain collector would be shot. One of the last acts of violence my grandfather remembers seeing was Yuri begging for his life as there was no grain left and nothing to collect. They shot him anyway, right in the head, in front of my grandfather.

At this point, Dido broke down sobbing, as he relived that cruelty. We hugged tightly through the tears.

Martin, who had never really understood the gravity of the Holodomor, saw our visible tears. He's only thirty years old, and of course he knew about the Holodomor, but he grew up in Kyiv and just heard stories. He never comprehended how anyone would have survived that madness, let alone live to tell people about it or come back and relive it.

What a painful day.

Peace,
H.

49

November 23

Dear Diary,

The day passed quickly, and maybe that's a good thing. We were all wiped and drained emotionally. Speaking was unnecessary. The drive back to our hotel last night was sooooooo long. It was dark when we arrived at our hotel. Washed up and straight to bed, appetites gone.

Staying in a hotel suite together to be near one another and give support was great, but we were worried about Dido.

Our last important remembrance is tomorrow – the fourth Saturday in November. We will visit, pray and remember the victims of the Holodomor, especially Dido's deceased family included in this memorial in Kyiv.

Dear diary, I can't sleep. Grandfather is in pain. I hope crying helps. I pray it does.

Peace,
H.

50

November 24

Dear Diary,

Fell asleep around 3 a.m. and way too soon, it's morning. We all had a restless sleep. We were zombies.

We decided to walk to Independence Square, also known as Maidan Square, and pay tribute to the "Heaven's Hundred." In February of 2014, after peacefully protesting Ukrainian government corruption, 100 protestors were killed by security forces. They were recognized posthumously by the government and given the "Order of the Heaven's Hundred Heroes" medals. The downfall of President Viktor Yanukovych was a victory to many Ukrainians, but it came at a high price. Another atrocity - one gets so tired of hearing these things. It makes me feel so overwhelmed at times.

When will it end? It's so frustrating and sad. So much death. All this fighting, killing and destruction, and for what?

Ukraine has a history of invasion by so many countries. There's this tale of a very old Ukrainian woman. Never moved. Born in her house, grew up in the same house, married and lived in this house her whole life, but had lived in five different countries: the Austro-Hungarian Empire, Poland, Germany, the USSR and now again Ukraine. Isn't that ridiculous?

Walking along the square, the sun was shining and there was a surprising amount of activity. Kyiv has a lot of outdoor and indoor markets selling beautiful wares and flowers. Ukrainians love kalyna, poppies and sunflowers. Ukrainians love to dress up as well sometimes using a combination of modern and traditional embroidered styles.

The square was filled with people shouting, "Remember the Holodomor!" It was loud. Travelling by cab, we went to see the Monument to the Victims of the Holodomor of 1932-33. The museum is on the Pecherska Hills on the right bank of the Dnipro River.

The remembrance service started promptly at 11 a.m. and continued throughout the day with many speakers and discussions, prayers and songs.

At night, we lit candles for the millions of souls lost. The entire area was packed, and we felt uplifted. We remembered and prayed for grandpa's mother and father and his two brothers and six sisters. Lit ten candles. As we lit them, Grandfather looked like an angel. His spirit soared. Through tears, my dearest Dido said he would never forget the Holodomor and his family. Millions of victims are not forgotten. And Ukrainian culture, traditions and language seem stronger than ever and, more importantly, Ukrainian spirits are united.

"Long live Ukraine!" many people shouted. "Long live the spirits of our ancestors!"

I was proud of Dido for stepping forward with his life and saying no to evil, his way of fighting back. As a child, he was helpless. Now an adult, he is a survivor, sharing his story. And my grandfather and I are solid. All my questions dragged him back in time, and brought back memories, but in the end, he's on a path to healing.

Today, diary, my grandfather Bohdan, my dearest Dido, looked at me with those big blue tear-filled eyes and said,

"Dyakuyu, my dove, I love you." He gave me the biggest smile and hug imaginable. It filled my heart completely.

"I knew we came to seek answers and the truth," said Dido. "The truth has set me free and there is great hope and healing for me and all of Ukraine."

With that, my dear diary, my dearest Dido raised his fist in the air, and joined in the chorus of shouts. "Long live Ukraine!"

And, being the proudest granddaughter in the world in that moment, I did the exact same.

Peace,
H.

Additional Author's Note

In 1992, my second cousin, Jennie Franko (née Dubyk) travelled to Ukraine with the Ukrainian Catholic Women's League of Canada (UCWLC) to meet her mother's family. Her mother was Ksenka Dubyk (née Hrabowa), born in western Ukraine, August 5, 1904 and died in Canada on June 8, 2007. Ksenka was from a family of nine children – six girls and three boys. Her brothers and sisters were Petro, Hanka, Natasia, Mariana, Vasyl, Sofi, Stefan, and Kaska. In Ukraine, Jennie met her mother's sister, Hanka (or Hanusia) Klimochko (née Hrabowa).

Ksenka was the only person from her family that immigrated to Canada. The reason she came to Canada was that she knew Vasyl (Bill) Dubyk, who was from the same village, and he offered to pay her way to Canada. He arrived in Canada in 1926. Ksenka came in 1928 and insisted on paying her own passage, as she said, she might not want to marry Bill when she arrived.

Vasyl was my grandfather, Stefan Dubyk's brother from Perespa, Sokal. My grandfather immigrated to Canada in 1911. My grandmother, Tessie Woznakowski from Zupkova, Sokal, immigrated in 1912 and the two were married in Canada in

1913. They had seven children; one of them was Sophie Mutala (née Dubyk), who was my mother.

One of the first stories Jennie's *Titka* Hanka (or Aunt Anna) told Jennie when she first met her in Ukraine was about the *Holodomor*. Hanka was married to a Mr. Klimochko and together they had five children: Marie, Ivan, Bohdan, Stefan, and Stefanie. One of the children was severely malnourished and had health problems from lack of food and nutrition.

Auntie Hanka said the soldiers came to her village in 1932 in Perespa, Sokal looking for food and killed any live animals. She had one cow and they shot it on the spot in front of her. She had a new-born and needed the cow's milk to feed her baby; she begged the soldiers not to shoot it, but they did anyway. After that, she had no milk to feed her baby.

Luckily, Hanka had hidden some sugar beets that the soldiers did not find and that's the only way they survived that winter. They cooked the sugar beets; the baby drank the juice and the rest of them ate the pulp. Hanka's husband was sent off to Siberia to work. She never saw him again. The older people in the village gave their food to children as they were concerned about them. The *Holodomor* started in eastern Ukraine but soon spread to central Ukraine. Today's western Ukraine (a part of Poland during the time of the *Holodomor*) did not experience the *Holodomor* directly.

TEACHING FACTS

1. What was the *Holodomor*?

Holodomor is a Ukrainian word that translates into "murder by starvation." It's the genocide that Soviet authorities, led by Joseph Stalin, carried out against Ukrainians in the early 1930s. It's believed that 10,000,000 Ukrainians died. The Government of Canada has recognized the fourth Saturday in November as the international day of remembrance for Ukrainians who perished during the *Holodomor*.

2. Why did the Soviet authorities starve Ukrainians?

Ukraine was forced to join the Soviet Union. Stalin wanted to get rid of "Ukrainian bourgeois nationalism." He arrested, deported and executed Ukrainian cultural, religious and political leaders in order to take complete control of Ukraine. Stalin's policy of collectivization and communism by the USSR and starvation of Ukrainians was his way of not losing Ukraine to independence and bringing Ukraine to its knees.

3. What was the collectivization of agriculture?

In the early 1930s, Stalin ordered the collectivization of agriculture or collective farms. The Soviet state owned everything. When Ukrainian farmers resisted the seizure of their property, they were forced into government collective farms. Stalin and his soldiers carried out the *Holodomor* to punish the Ukrainian farmers and to get rid of opposition to collectivization and Soviet rule.

4. How was the *Holodomor* carried out?

Stalin and his soldiers set grain quotas for Ukrainian farmers. The leaders took all grain, even the seeds. Communist troops searched individual houses, taking wheat and food, leaving the people hungry.

USSR sold millions of tonnes of wheat to western countries during the *Holodomor*. Soldiers closed the borders so starving victims could not leave and forbade them from leaving villages or coming to cities to find food.

5. What was the impact of the *Holodomor?*

Ukrainians died at the rate of 30,000 per day in June 1933. One in four Ukrainians starved to death in the Ukrainian countryside. The 1937 Soviet census showed a sharp decrease in the Ukrainian population. Stalin shot anyone who allowed census information to be released or released it themselves. For more than fifty years, Soviets denied the *Holodomor*. Even today, Russian leader Vladimir Putin and his government still deny it.

6. Why is it important to teach people today about the *Holodomor?*

So, history doesn't repeat itself. And to honour the memory of millions of innocent people who lost their lives.

7. What is the definition of a genocide?

The definition of genocide in the Geneva Convention as it stands today is based on four constituent parts:

1. A criminal act
2. With the intention of destroying
3. A national, ethnic or religious group
4. Targeted as such

8. Based on the above definition, what are other genocides that have occurred in the world?

- Ismail Enver (Ottoman Turkey, 1915)
- Adolf Hitler (Holocaust-Germany 1939-1945)
- Kayumba Nyamwasa (Rwanda, 1994-97)

9. Who are the four men on the cover of the book and what is their significance to the *Holodomor?*

From left to right they are Karl Marx, Friedrich Engels, Vladimir Lenin, Joseph Stalin. This image was very popular during the spread of communism and was placed on posters and propaganda materials to promote communism.

GLOSSARY OF UKRAINIAN WORDS

Baba - (bah-bah) old woman, grandmother

Babushka – (bah-bush-kah) Ukrainian headscarf, and term of endearment

Batko - (baht-ko) father

Bohdan - (Boh -dan) God-given or gift from God

Bozhe – (Bo-zhe) my God

Braty – (brah-tee) brothers

Chai – (ch-i) tea

Dekulakization – (dee-koo-lahk-i-zay-shun) Stalin tried to get rid of kulaks. The Soviet campaign of political repressions, arrests, deportations, and executions of millions of wealthy peasants and their families in the 1929-33 period of the first five-year plan when the *Holodomor* took place.

Dido - (dyee-doh) grandfather

Dyakuyu - (dyak-koo-yoo) thank you

Holod - (huh-lud) famine or hunger

Holubka – (huh-loob-ka) a derivative of holub, the Ukrainian word for dove, used as dear, darling, loved one

Holodomor - (huh-luh-duh-more) death by forced starvation

Holub - (huh-loob) dove

Kalyna – (kah-ly-nah) cranberry

Kolach – (koh-lahch) Ukrainian bread, circular shaped

Kolhosp – (kol-hosp) Ukrainian acronym for 'collective farm' property

Kulak(s) - (koo- lawk) wealthy peasant farmer – Russian word

Kurkul(s) - (ker-kool)- wealthy peasant farmer/Ukrainian word

Kyiv Pecherska Lavra – (Ky-yeev) (Pe-cher-ska) (Lav-rah) known as the Kyiv Monastery of the Caves, an active historic Orthodox Christian monastery

Mator zhenyko – (ma-tor) (zhe-ny-koh) patties made from weeds and crushed straw

Moryty – (muh-ry-ty) torment

Opir and Stryi Rivers – (O-peer) (Stree) There is a legend that the Ukrainian "Robin Hood," Oleksa Dovbush was wounded, and his blood stained the riverbank causing the red rocks that can be seen there.

Oy bozhe - (oy) (bo-zhe) oh God

Panakhyda – (pah-nah-khy-dah) a short funeral or requiem prayer

Parastas – (pah-rah-stahs) a solemn funeral or requiem prayer service for the dead

Pecherska (Kyiv Metro) – (Pe-cher-skah) one of the stations of the underground metro near the Pecheseska Lavra

Pecherska Lavra – (Pe-cher-skah) (Lahv-rah) Kyiv Pechersk Lavra or Kyiv Pechersk Lavra, also known as the Kyiv Monastery of the Caves, an active historic Orthodox Christian monastery

Pyrohy - (peh-roh-heh) stuffed dumplings, sometimes called varenyky or perogy

Petras de – (pet-rahs) (de) gates of

Poods – (poods) a measurement for grain approximately 16.38 kilograms (36.11 pounds). It was used in Russia, Belarus, and Ukraine.

Sertse - (ser-tse) my heart

Sestry – (ses-trey) sisters

Soloveyko – (so-luh-vay-koh) nightingale

Tak - (tahk)-yes; that's right

Tato - (tah-to) father

Titka - (teet-ka) aunt

Torgsins – (Torg-sins) Russian- named stores and acronym for trade with foreigners

Varenyky - (vah-re-neh-key) stuffed dumplings, boiled

Vichnaya pamiat – (veech-nah-yah) (pahm-yat) memory eternal

Verkhovna Rada – (Ver-khoh-nah) (Rah-dah) Ukrainian parliament

TIMELINE

1917

Ukraine fought and gained independence. The Soviet Red Army took over Ukrainian forces. The Bolsheviks, led by Vladimir Lenin, took over in Russia.

1922

The Soviet Union by force makes Ukraine one of the republics of the USSR.

1924

After Lenin's death, Joseph Stalin took over the Soviet Union. Stalin wanted Ukraine and tried to get rid of Ukrainian national culture.

1928

Stalin's policy of collectivisation took farmer's private land, equipment and livestock. Stalin forced farmers to work on collective farms and sold grain to western countries to finance his five-year plan for communism and industrialization.

1929

Independent Ukrainian farmers refused to join collective farms. Stalin started "class warfare" against farmers who owned their land or the *kulaks* (*kurkuls*, in Ukrainian) He sent troops and secret police to "liquidate them as a class." Stalin shot or deported anyone who resists.

1930

1.5 million Ukrainians were victims to Stalin's "dekulakization" policies, to eliminate *kulaks*. Armed soldiers took land, livestock and other property, and evicted families. Close to half a million people in Ukraine were packed into trains, sent to Siberia. With no food or shelter, many people died.

1932-1933

Soviet government increased Ukraine's grain quotas. Starvation occurred. In the summer of 1932, Stalin called for the arrest or execution of any person who took as little as a few stalks of wheat or food from fields. People were not allowed to leave the villages and young soldiers were sent to take anything edible.

1933

By June, people in Ukraine died at the rate of 30,000 a day; nearly a third of them were children under 10. Between 1932 and 1933, four million deaths occurred because of starvation. Deportations, executions, or deaths from ordinary causes were not included in this number. Stalin denied any famine in Ukraine. He exported millions of tons of grain to the Western world for money and eliminated anyone that disagreed with him.

SUPPRESSION AND RECOGNITION

OF THE *HOLODOMOR*

"Any report of a famine in Russia is today an exaggeration or malignant propaganda. There is no actual starvation or deaths from starvation but there is widespread mortality from diseases due to malnutrition." *(Reported by the New York Times correspondent and Pulitzer-prize winner Walter Duranty)*

Western journalists like Walter Duranty denied the famine. The Soviet Union refused Western help with the famine. Stalin said the claim of the famine was anti-Soviet propaganda.

In November 1933, the United States, under newly elected president Franklin D. Roosevelt, recognized Stalin's Communist government with a new trade deal. In 1934, the West allowed the Soviet Union into the League of Nations and ignored the famine to trade with the Soviet Union. Stalin's Five-Year Plan for the modernization of USSR was dependent on goods and technology from the West.

Ukrainian groups sought acknowledgment of this tragic, massive genocide. However, it wasn't until the late 1980s, with the publication of Robert Conquest's "Harvest of Sorrow," the report of the US Commission on the Ukraine Famine, review of the International Commission of Inquiry into the 1932–33 Famine in Ukraine, and the release of the documentary "Harvest of Despair," that the world becomes aware. In Soviet Ukraine, of course, the *Holodomor* was kept hidden. Shortly before Ukraine became independent in 1991 and the fall of the Soviet Union, archives were opened. Suppressed oral testimony of *Holodomor* survivors in Ukraine was obtained and evidence and proof of Ukraine's famine and genocide of the 1930s was finally recognized.

Recognition by Ukraine and the World

On November 28, 2006, The *Verkhovna Rada* (Parliament of Ukraine) passed a decree defining the *Holodomor* as a deliberate Act of Genocide. Although the Russian government continues to call Ukraine's depiction of the famine a "one-sided falsification of history," it's recognized as a genocide by approximately two dozen nations and is now the focus of considerable international research and documentation.

Recognition by the Government of Saskatchewan

On May 7, 2008, Saskatchewan became the first province in Canada to recognize the *Holodomor* as an act of genocide through the passage of Bill 40, introduced by Deputy Premier Ken Krawetz. Bill 40 was enacted to recognize the Ukrainian famine and genocide; the fourth Saturday in November each year is enshrined and recognized as the "Ukrainian Famine and Genocide (*Holodomor*) Memorial Day."

Full text of Bill 40: www.qp.gov.sk.ca/documents/english/FirstRead/2007-08/Bill-40.pdf

Recognition by the Government of Canada and Provinces

In May of 2008, Canada was among the leading nations to recognize the *Holodomor* as an act of genocide. In addition to the Federal Government, four Canadian provinces have also recognized the *Holodomor*, proclaiming the fourth Saturday of each November as *Holodomor* Remembrance Day in Canada. These days noted were:

Federal Government of Canada – May 29, 2008

Province of Saskatchewan – May 7, 2008

Province of Alberta – October 30, 2008

Province of Manitoba – December 4, 2008

Province of Ontario – April 9, 2009

Remember

(I was filled with such deep emotion while researching and writing this book about the *Holodomor*, I was moved to write this song - Marion Mutala)

Remember, remember the Holodomor
Remember, remember the Holodomor

Hear, hear the church bells ringing
Tolling for justice for ten million lives

Look, look at the candles burning brightly
Stars shining from heaven for souls that were lost

Remember, remember the Holodomor
Remember, remember the Holodomor

Listen, listen hear the cries of the children
Feed me, I'm starving, voices never heard

Touch, touch the wounds on their bodies
Feel, feel their painful broken hearts

Remember, remember the Holodomor
Remember, remember the Holodomor

Fives ears of grain, victims of Stalin
Ukrainian remains turned to dust

To mourn the Holodomor is respectful
But to remember the Holodomor is holy

Remember, remember the Holodomor
Remember, remember the Holodomor
Remember, remember the Holodomor

Lyrics @2018 Marion Mutala

The Bard of Ukraine
(March 9, 1814-March 10, 1861)

(I wrote this poem to recognize and celebrate the 200ᵗʰ anniversary of Taras Shevchenko's birth. He was known as the "Bard of Ukraine" - Marion Mutala)

Taras Shevchenko, we remember
Peasant's son, orphaned at eleven
Unschooled layman
Cultured serf

We remember your freedom
One of life's small victories

We remember how you suffered for the love of humanity
And how you spoke as a wandering minstrel in Kobzar
Gave us testament in Zapovit

We remember a literary genius,
Great humanitarian, poet, artist speaking through one thousand works of art

We remember your death
Free or serf, slave or not
Your voice resonates from the grave, continual shout for fairness, justice,
equality in the world

End oppression
Eliminate poverty, share wealth
Take care of woman, children, especially the orphans

We remember your compassion and prayers for Ukrainian people
All people
All of humanity

Greed rampant
Leaders silent
Governments deaf
No one listened to your cries then or now
But still… we remember

Stop selfishness
Stop war

And…we will always remember
And pay tribute to your ideas, beliefs and vision
Create peace
Hope
Create a new and better world

Today, tomorrow and always…

NOTES

Beginning Quote

1. Eyewitness account of survivor N. Mychajlowska (age 11 in 1933). http://education.holodomor.ca/teaching-materials/N

Chapter Three

1. Polikarp Kybkalo was a Genocide Survivor who testified before the United States Ukraine Famine Commission in Washington, DC on October 8, 1986. http://ncua.inform-decisions.com/eng /files/UkrGenocide_Teacher_Student_Workbook.pdf.
2. *Europe's black hole.* Article written by Robert Fulford, originally published in *The New York Times* (March 30, 1933). Later republished in the *Saskatoon Star Phoenix* (April 2, 2016).
3. Pyrih, Ruslan, and Stephen Bandera. *Holodomor of 1932-33 in Ukraine: Documents and Materials* (2008).
   a. William Strang on September 26th, 1933 while at the British Embassy in Moscow (page 109).
   b. Stanislaw Kosior's (Secretary of the Politburo, the Communist Party of Ukraine) letter to Stalin in April 1932 (pages 20–21).
4. Journalist George Santayana describing the restrictions on reporting the Holodomor. https://www.theatlantic.com/ international/archive/2017/10/red-famine-anne-applebaum-ukraine-soviet-union/542610

Chapter Five

1. *Spreading Story of Ukrainian Genocide.* Article written by Darlene Polachic in the *Saskatoon Star Phoenix*, August 27, 2016.
2. *Europe's black hole.* Article written by Robert Fulford, originally published in *The New York Times* (March 30, 1933). Later republished in the *Saskatoon Star Phoenix* (April 2, 2016).

3. Eyewitness account of Antonina Meleshchenko, a resident of the village of Kosivka, region of Kyiv. http:// holodomorct.org/ holodomor-survivor-eyewitness-accounts/

Chapter Six

1. *Spreading Story of Ukrainian Genocide.* Article written by Darlene Polachic in the *Saskatoon Star Phoenix,* August 27, 2016.
2. Franko, Roma Z., Morris, Sonia V., Zvychayna Olena, Hutsalo Yevhen, and Dimarov, Anatoliy. *A Hunger Most Cruel: Selected Prose Fiction.* (2002) page 75.

Chapter Seven

1. *Europe's black hole.* Article written by Robert Fulford, originally published in *The New York Times* (March 30, 1933). Later republished in the *Saskatoon Star Phoenix* (April 2, 2016).

Chapter Nine

1. *Spreading Story of Ukrainian Genocide.* Article written by Darlene Polachic, the *Saskatoon Star Phoenix,* August 27, 2016.
2. Stalin's opinion of Ukrainians resistance to communism. http://www.ucrdc.org/HA-ENEMY_OF_THE_PEOPLE.html
3. Applebaum, Anne. *Red Famine–Stalin's War on Ukraine* (2017) page 52 and 86.
4. Romanyschyn, Oleh, Steciw, Orest, and Gregorovich, Andrew. *Special Publication: Holodomor-The Ukrainian Genocide January 2nd, 1933.* League of Ukrainian Canadians Ukrainian Research Institute (2014) page 122.

Chapter Ten

1. *Ukraine Remembers – the World Acknowledges.* Article in the *Saskatoon Star Phoenix.* November 21, 2016.

2. Romanyschyn, Oleh, Steciw, Orest, and Gregorovich, Andrew. *Special Publication Holodomor-The Ukrainian Genocide 1932-1933*. League of Ukrainian Canadians Ukrainian Research Institute, (2014) page 36.

Chapter Twelve

1. Eyewitness account of survivor Yar Slavutych. *Holodomor: Voices of Survivors*, a documentary by Producer/Director Ariadna Ochrymovych, Black Sea Media Inc. (2015).

Chapter Fifteen

1. *Spreading Story of Ukrainian Genocide*. Article written by Darlene Polachic, the Saskatoon Star Phoenix, August 27, 2016.
2. Applebaum, Anne. *Red Famine–Stalin's War on Ukraine*. (2017) page 242.

Chapter Seventeen

1. Romanyschyn, Oleh, Steciw, Orest, and Gregorovich, Andrew. *Special Publication Holodomor-The Ukrainian Genocide 1932-1933*. League of Ukrainian Canadians Ukrainian Research Institute. (2014) page 28.
2. The meeting of the two rivers in Ukraine. https://www.revolvy.com/main/index.php?s=Stryi+River

Chapter Eighteen

1. Applebaum, Anne. *Red Famine–Stalin's War on Ukraine*. (2017) page 187.
2. *Europe's black hole*. Article written by Robert Fulford, originally published in *The New York Times* (March 30, 1933). Later republished in the *Saskatoon Star Phoenix* (April 2, 2016).

Chapter Nineteen

1. Applebaum, Anne. *Red Famine–Stalin's War on Ukraine*. (2017) page 198.

Chapter Twenty

1. Mother Theresa words of wisdom. www.goodreads. com/quotes/6946-not-all-of-us-can-do-great-things-but-we and http://www.catholicnews.com /services/ englishnews/2016/mother-teresa-do-small-things-with greatlove.cfm.
2. Romanyschyn, Oleh, Steciw, Orest, and Gregorovich, Andrew. *Special Publication Holodomor-The Ukrainian Genocide 1932-1933*. League of Ukrainian Canadians Ukrainian Research Institute. (2014) cover.
3. Applebaum, Anne. *Red Famine–Stalin's War on Ukraine*. (2017) page 263.

Chapter Twenty-One

1. Applebaum, Anne. *Red Famine–Stalin's War on Ukraine*. (2017) page 264.

Chapter Twenty-Two

1. Hanna Doroshenko, a survivor, called the Holodomor a "bloodless war". http://holodomorct.org/holodomor-survivor-eyewitness-accounts/

Chapter Thirty-Five

1. Applebaum, Anne. *Red Famine–Stalin's War on Ukraine*. (2017) pages 355-356.
2. Hoffman, David Lloyd. *Stalinist Values: The Cultural Norms of Soviet Modernity, 1917-1941* (2013) page 144.
3. Pyrih, Ruslan, and Stephen Bandera. *Holodomor of 1932-33 in Ukraine: Documents and Materials*. (2008).

BIBLIOGRAPHY

Books

Applebaum, Anne. *Red Famine–Stalin's War on Ukraine*. Toronto: Signal, 2017.

Dolot, Miron. *Execution by Hunger -The Hidden Holocaust*. New York-London: W.W. Norton & Company.1985.

Franko, Roma Z., Morris, Sonia V., Zvychayna Olena, Hutsalo Yevhen, and Dimarov, Anatoliy. *A Hunger Most Cruel: Selected Prose Fiction*. Winnipeg: Language Lanterns Publications, 2002.

Hoffman, David Lloyd. *Stalinist Values: The Cultural Norms of Soviet Modernity, 1917-1941*. Cornell University Press, 2003.

Powers, Eugenia Maleschok. *EEVAHN Child of the Holodomor*, Canada: Antecedent Publishers, 2013.

Pyrih, Ruslan, and Stephen Bandera. *Holodomor of 1932-33 in Ukraine: Documents and Materials*. Kyiv: Kyiv Mohyla Academy Publishing Press, 2008.

Romanyschyn, Oleh, Steciw, Orest, and Gregorovich, Andrew. *Special Publication Holodomor-The Ukrainian Genocide 1932-1933* Toronto: League of Ukrainian Canadians Ukrainian Research Institute, 2014.

Documentaries

Holodomor: Voices of Survivors, a documentary by Producer/Director Ariadna Ochrymovych, DVD, Black Sea Media Inc. 2015.

Harvest of Despair: The 1932-33 Famine in Ukraine. Toronto: Ukrainian Canadian Research and Documentation Centre, 1984. (Probes the causes and consequences of the Soviet engineered genocidal famine. Features eighteen interviews with survivors and witnesses, including: Lev Kopelev, a former Soviet activist; British journalist Malcolm Muggeridge; and former Soviet General Petro Grigorenko).

Print Media

Europe's Black Hole. Article written by Robert Fulford, *Saskatoon Star Phoenix,* April 2, 2016, page NP6.

1932/33-Holodomor - Commemorations of the Ukrainian Famine-Genocide. Saskatoon Star Phoenix, November 23, 2015, pages B5, B6, B7, B8.

Spreading Story of Ukrainian Genocide. Article written by Darlene Polachic, quote by Holly Paluck, *Saskatoon Star Phoenix,* August 27, 2016, Page D10.

Stage Drama

Evanko, Father Edward Danylo, *Murder by Starvation,* 2015.

Websites

http://www.holodomorsurvivors.ca/Survivors.html

http://blogs.bu.edu/guidedhistory/russia-and-its-empires/elise-alexander

http://education.holodomor.ca/teaching-materials/

https://www.investukraine.net/agriculture/bread-basket-of-europe

http://faminegenocide.com/resources/was_it_holodomor.htm

http://www.holodomor.ca

http://holodomor.ca/education/teaching-materials

http://www.holodomorct.org/index.html

http://www.holodomorsurvivors.ca/Survivors.html

http://www.merchantamerica.com/holocaustsurvivor/

https://www.hoover.org/research/enemy-state

https://www.marxists.org/reference/archive/stalin/works/decades-index.htm

https://www.marxists.org/archive/lenin/works/1918/may/22b.htm

http://ncua.inform-decisions.com/eng/files/UkrGenocide_Teacher_Student_Workbook.pdf.

https://www.revolvy.com/main/index.php?s=Order

https://www.revolvy.com/main/index.php?s=Stryi+River

https://www.theatlantic.com/international/archive/2017/10/red-famine-anne-applebaum-ukraine-soviet-union/542610

www.qp.gov.sk.ca/documents/english/FirstRead/2007-08/Bill-40.pdf

http://www.ucrdc.org

http://www.un.org/en/genocideprevention/genocide.html

https:// www.voicesintoaction.ca

Teaching the Holodomor

Holodomor national Awareness Tour and Mobile Classroom www.holodomortour.ca or holodomor.tour@cufoundation.ca -620 Spading Ave. Toronto, Ontario 1-416-966-9800

Voices into Action https://www.voicesintoaction.ca

ACKNOWLEDGEMENTS

Thank you to Arthur Slade, Angie Wollbaum, and Larry Mikulcik for their wisdom, feedback and guidance.

Much gratitude and love to Dr. Bill Gulka for his Ukrainian translations and editing assistance.

Thank you as well to Martin Hryniuk, Jacquie Moore and Zoé Beaulieu-Prpick for their editing expertise.

Thank you to Olha Tkachenko for her original graphics for the cover and inside content.

Thank you to Anne Applebaum for her amazing research and documentation on the Holodomor. Her book, *Red Famine*, is a wonderful source for anyone who wishes to learn more about this tragic period of Ukrainian history.

 UKRAINIAN CANADIAN CONGRESS
Saskatchewan Provincial Council

The author gratefully acknowledges funding
from the Ukrainian Canadian Congress's
(Saskatchewan Provincial Council) Hromada Legacy Fund.

(In 2014, the Hromada Legacy Fund of Saskatchewan was launched to pay homage to the Ukrainian community's roots and heritage while reflecting its unique cultural identity.)

ABOUT THE AUTHOR

Marion Mutala has a master's degree in educational administration and taught school in the K-12 system for 30 years. She has a passion for the arts and loves to write, sing, play guitar, travel and read.

Marion is the author of the national bestselling and award-winning children's books: *Baba's Babushka: A Magical Ukrainian Christmas, Baba's Babushka: A Magical Ukrainian Easter, Baba's Babushka: A Magical Ukrainian Wedding* and *Kohkum's Babushka: A Magical Métis/ Ukrainian Tale.* She is also the author of *Grateful, The Time for Peace is Now, Ukrainian Daughter's Dance* (a poetry collection), *More Baba's, Please!* and *My Buddy, Dido!*
Marion's awards for her children's books include:

~ **Baba's Babushka: A Magical Ukrainian Christmas**
   Recipient of: The Anna Pidruchney Award (2010)

~ **Baba's Babushka: A Magical Ukrainian Easter**
   Nominated for: Saskatchewan Book Award – Publishing in Education (2013)

~ **Baba's Babushka: A Magical Ukrainian Wedding**
   Recipient of: High Plains Book Award - Best Children's Book (2014)

~ **My Buddy, Dido!**
   Nominated for: High Plains Book Award - Best Children's Book (2019)

My Dearest Dido - The Holodomor Story is Marion Mutala's eleventh book. Visit her website at: www.babasbabushka.ca to learn more.

Baba's Babushka:
A Magical Ukrainian Wedding
Recipient of: High Plains Book Award –
Best Children's Book (2014)

"An engrossing picture book, rendered in beautiful detail by author Marion Mutala and artist Amber Rees, that tells the heartwarming tale of a young woman named Natalia. Natalia, aided by the memory of her grandmother, goes on a magical journey to learn more about her family's – and people's – rich history. During Natalia's walk down memory lane, she visits all the important moments which involved her grandparents' time together as young people. The story details her grandparents' courtship, including the meeting of their two families before and during their seven-day Ukrainian wedding. Mutala uniquely and accurately depicts the Ukrainian customs that are special to a couple's wedding."

"Mutala's accurate portrayal of these customs will speak volumes to readers both familiar and unfamiliar with them. Her playful dialogue between the large cast of characters runs through everything, sprinkled with Ukrainian words and their meaning. Through this, she demonstrates a love of and desire to preserve the Ukrainian way of life."

Above comments from SaskBooks Review April 2014

ISBN: 9781927756065 (Published by: Your Nickel's Worth Publishing)

More Babas, Please!

"More Babas, Please! is a happy celebration of grandmothers. All grandmothers everywhere. 'Big ones, small ones, fat ones, tall. Curly-haired, straight-haired, wig-wearing, bald.' The rhyming has an almost sing-song rhythm which seems so natural that you instinctively know that a lot of work has gone into making it seem so effortless! The layout is classic and clean with lots of white space and large type, perfect for early readers and grown-ups with bad eyesight. Each left page features a beautiful full page colour illustration by Ukrainian-born illustrator Olha Tkachenko. The book gave me a warm feeling as I reflected on my own grandmother. It speaks to all the good that grandmothers do (and are) and to all the ways they surround their grandchildren with love, understanding, acceptance, affection and food!"

Comments from SaskBooks Book Review May 2017

ISBN: 9781927756928 (Published by: Your Nickel's Worth Publishing)

My Buddy, Dido!
Nominated for: High Plains Book Award –
Best Children's Book (2019)

"Grandfathers are amazing people. Whether they play games, tell jokes, read stories, or simply snuggle their grandchildren, they are always sharing their love. In this delightful picture book, Mutala reminds us why grandpas are such exceptional family members."

"With her background in Ukrainian children's tales … Mutala has a great grasp of the fundamentals, introducing readers to Dido, the Ukrainian grandfather. Before the tale even starts, a full-page graphic showcases 'grandpa' in other languages with bright, bold colours."

"Marion also strays from the regular story format, choosing instead to go over a Dido's characteristics in rhyming verses: "Who listens to me when I'm mad? Who consoles me when I'm sad? Who has time when I'm in a pickle or when I'm ready for a tickle?" Every facet of a grandfather is explored in poetry sure to appeal both the young and old."

Comments from SaskBooks review August 2018.

ISBN: 9781988783239 (Published by: Your Nickel's Worth Publishing)

Kohkum's Babushka: A Magical Métis/Ukrainian Tale

This is a tale about two diverse families and their first encounter with one another. It shows the beauty of their differences and similarities, particularly the generosity and reciprocity valued by each family's cultural tradition. Through another magical Babushka, Marion Mutala takes readers into a vibrant Prairie world that weaves fact and fantasy to witness two families, one Métis and the other Ukrainian, meeting for the first time. Through this magical encounter, we see core values intrinsic to our common humanity: our curiosity and empathy, and our willingness to share with others, regardless of language or culture.

ISBN: 978192679578-2 (Published by: Gabriel Dumont Institute Press)

50

Baba's Babushka: A Magical Ukrainian Easter
Nominated for: Saskatchewan Book Award –
Publishing in Education (2013)

"This enchanting sequel to the award-winning Baba's Babushka: A Magical Ukrainian Christmas is sure to delight Marion Mutala's many fans. This time it's spring, and we join Natalia as she is once again swept magically away to a far-off land for another uniquely Ukrainian adventure.

Natalia is sent outside while the paska, the Easter bread her mother is baking, rises. She's meant to be collecting the eggs but instead finds herself reflecting on her beloved Baba, her grandmother, who has recently died. Suddenly she feels raindrops brush her cheeks. The raindrops turn into a babushka that covers her hair and then she's off... "up and away, high in the sky... racing through time and space". Natalia finds herself in a crowd of people in the early morning in front of a village church. It's Easter and Natalia is caught up in the celebrations as she joins the procession of people carrying candles..."

The book is easy-to-read with beautiful full-page illustrations by Saskatchewan illustrator Wendy Siemens.

Comments from SaskBooks review April 2013.

ISBN: 978-1894431705 (Published by: Your Nickel's Worth Publishing)

Baba's Babushka: A Magical Ukrainian Christmas
Recipient of: The Anna Pidruchney Award (2010)

'Saskatchewan author Marion Mutala has created a charming story that celebrates her proud Ukrainian heritage and lives up to the subtitle of her book, 'A Magical Ukrainian Christmas'. Natalia, the star of this lively story, is a little Ukrainian girl living in rural Saskatchewan who is taken, with the reader, on an enchanted journey back in time. Although Natalia is excited, like all children, about Christmas, her joy is marred by a deep sadness. This will be the first Christmas that her beloved grandmother, Baba, will not be present to share in the fun, festivities, and traditions of Christmas with her family. One day, a brightly coloured red and blue babushka, or headscarf, appears out of nowhere that reminds Natalia of the one her Baba used to wear. Mysteriously transported to another time and place, Natalia finds herself sharing a meal with a strangely familiar family who perform all the same Christmas Eve traditions her own family does.... Natalia is just as magically transported back to the present and her own home.... She finds a picture of her Baba on the table beside her bed with the red and blue babushka tucked underneath it. Who was the little girl she spent Christmas Eve with? Could it have been her own dear Baba?"

Comments from SaskBooks review January 2011.

ISBN: 9781894431538 (Published by: Your Nickel's Worth Publishing)

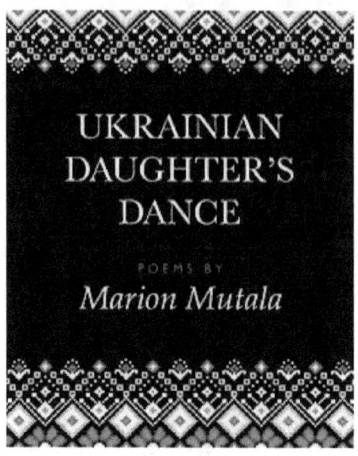

Ukrainian Daughter's Dance

The rich and varied poems in Ukrainian Daughter's Dance speak to the heart as they document a woman's life journey, as a Ukrainian-Canadian, and as a prairie woman, and her voyage of self-discovery. Her story can be anyone's story. Poems explore issues of immigrant identity and voice in the prairies, and celebrate a cultural heritage expressed through song, dance, art, work and life.

ISBN: 9781771333337 (Published by: Inanna Publications)

ABOUT THE ARTIST

Ukrainian-born **Olha Tkachenko** is the artist behind the inside and cover art of *My Dearest Dido*. She was also the illustrator for two previous books by Marion Mutala: *More Babas, Please!* and *My Buddy, Dido!*

Since 2008, Olha has worked as a freelance children's illustrator and has created many children books in the USA, Canada, and Russia.

In 2014, Olha and her family moved to Canada, where she worked at the Ukrainian Museum of Canada in Saskatchewan and led a private art school. Her work has been exhibited in Ukraine, France, and Canada.

Olha works with various media such as oil, soft pastel, watercolors, and batiks. Her hot batik works combine traditional Ukrainian technique of Pysankas (painted Easter Eggs) and modern concepts.

Reviewers have stated that Tkachenko adds a fantastical element to the stories she illustrates with her watercolour inspired illustrations. SaskBook reviewers claim her "simplicity and splashes of colour are both childlike and detailed, an absolute necessity if you want to hold your reader's attention".

Olha says, *"I love tales where a line between reality and imagination is almost erased, like in childhood. If we ask children about miracles, they might deny this idea, but even the desire to look smart and adult would not stop a child from peering into the grass near the path to see a gnome or a fairy.*

Likewise, I love peering into reality looking for a mystery. This is why I'd call my style realistic fantasy. My favourite medium - coloured pencils - expresses my feelings in the best way. My drawings are full of colours and air. They breathe and the white light leaks out through the net of small pencil strokes just as grace is tangible through the ordinary things in our habitual, material world."

Find out more about her work at: https://www.olyaillustrations.com or www.olya-t.art

www.ingramcontent.com/pod-product-compliance
Lightning Source LLC
Chambersburg PA
CBHW070034260626
47159CB00005B/2037